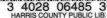
3 4028 06485 3
HARRIS COUNTY PUBLIC LIB

D1311944

JPIC Shulma
Shulman, Lisa
Over in the meadow at the
   big ballet

                    $16.99
              ocm62755483
              06/28/2007

Over in the Meadow at the Big Ballet

BY **Lisa Shulman**

ILLUSTRATED BY **Sarah Massini**

G. P. Putnam's Sons

G. P. PUTNAM'S SONS
A division of Penguin Young Readers Group. Published by The Penguin Group.
Penguin Group (USA) Inc., 375 Hudson Street, New York, NY 10014, U.S.A.
Penguin Group (Canada), 90 Eglinton Avenue East, Suite 700, Toronto, Ontario, Canada M4P 2Y3
(a division of Pearson Penguin Canada Inc.).
Penguin Books Ltd, 80 Strand, London WC2R 0RL, England.
Penguin Ireland, 25 St. Stephen's Green, Dublin 2, Ireland (a division of Penguin Books Ltd.).
Penguin Group (Australia), 250 Camberwell Road, Camberwell, Victoria 3124, Australia
(a division of Pearson Australia Group Pty Ltd).
Penguin Books India Pvt Ltd, 11 Community Centre, Panchsheel Park, New Delhi - 110 017, India.
Penguin Group (NZ), Cnr Airborne and Rosedale Roads, Albany, Auckland 1310, New Zealand
(a division of Pearson New Zealand Ltd).
Penguin Books (South Africa) (Pty) Ltd, 24 Sturdee Avenue, Rosebank, Johannesburg 2196, South Africa.
Penguin Books Ltd, Registered Offices: 80 Strand, London WC2R 0RL, England.

Text copyright © 2007 by Lisa Shulman. Illustrations copyright © 2007 by Sarah Massini. All rights reserved.
This book, or parts thereof, may not be reproduced in any form without permission in writing from the publisher,
G. P. Putnam's Sons, a division of Penguin Young Readers Group, 345 Hudson Street, New York, NY 10014.
G. P. Putnam's Sons, Reg. U.S. Pat. & Tm. Off. The scanning, uploading and distribution of this book via the Internet
or via any other means without the permission of the publisher is illegal and punishable by law.
Please purchase only authorized electronic editions, and do not participate in or encourage electronic piracy of
copyrighted materials. Your support of the author's rights is appreciated. The publisher does not have any control over
and does not assume any responsibility for author or third-party websites or their content.

Published simultaneously in Canada. Manufactured in China by South China Printing Co. Ltd.
Design by Marikka Tamura. Text set in Fontesque Sans. The art was painted using ink, acrylic and oil on paper.
Library of Congress Cataloging-in-Publication Data
Shulman, Lisa. Over in the meadow at the big ballet / by Lisa Shulman ; illustrated by Sarah Massini. p. cm.
Summary: A nervous little swan, a demanding teacher, and others work hard to prepare for a ballet recital.
[1. Dance recitals—Fiction. 2. Swans—Fiction. 3. Ballet—Fiction. 4. Stories in rhyme.]
I. Massini, Sarah, ill. II. Title. PZ8.3.S55975Ove 2007 [E]—dc22 2005034707 ISBN 978-0-399-24289-2
10 9 8 7 6 5 4 3 2 1
FIRST IMPRESSION

For my sisters, Corinne and Adrienne.—L. S.

For Shona and Maurice, little swans both.—S. M.

Over in the meadow where the dragonflies play
Stepped a nervous little swan and her teacher, Miss Faye.

"Onstage?"
asked the swan.

"That's right!"
said Miss Faye.

So they started getting ready for next week's ballet.

Early the next morning by the pond so blue
Frisked a quick little squirrel and her fluffy-tailed crew.

"Paint!"
said Miss Faye.

"We paint!"
said the crew.

So they painted a great castle and the stage set grew.

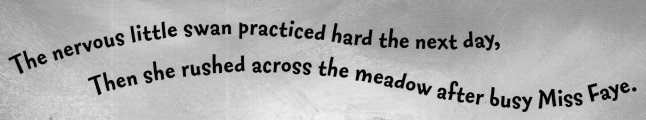

The nervous little swan practiced hard the next day,
Then she rushed across the meadow after busy Miss Faye.

"I can't!"
said the swan.

"You can!"
said Miss Faye.

So she danced even harder while her friends went to play.

Underneath the oak trees where the dirt road bends
Sewed a roly-poly hedgehog and her prickly hedgehog friends.

"Stitch!"
said Miss Faye.

"We stitch!"
said the friends.

So they stitched and they snipped through the long weekend.

The nervous little swan worried more each day
As she tried to explain to the elegant Miss Faye.

"I'll trip!"
said the swan.

"You'll dance!"
said Miss Faye.

But the swan wished she'd never even heard of ballet.

Under weeping willows by the pond in the grass
Stretched a green speckled frog and the dancers in her class.

"Bend!"
said Miss Faye.

"We bend!"
said the class.

So they bent and they stretched by the pond in the grass.

The nervous little swan tried to hide from Miss Faye
By the blackberry bushes where the wild roses sway.

"I'm sick!"
said the swan.

"You're fine!"
said Miss Faye.

So they had a quick rehearsal before the big day.

On the evening of the show near a flat gray rock
Dressed a plump white goose and the rest of her flock.

"Squeeze!"
said Miss Faye.

"We squeeze!"
said the flock.

So they squeezed and they laced and they preened by the rock.

The nervous little swan nearly fainted dead away

As she quaked behind the curtains next to watchful Miss Faye.

"I'm scared,"
said the swan.

"So am I!"
said Miss Faye.

"Before the curtains rise, I always feel the same way."

The startled little swan didn't know what to say;
Did every other dancer also feel this way?

The brave little swan watched the curtains slide away
As she stepped toward the stage and away from Miss Faye.

"I'm ready,"
said the swan.

"I know,"
said Miss Faye.

And they smiled at each other as the orchestra played.

Under the stage lights in a cape of chiffon
Spun the smiling little swan with her worries all gone.

"Leap!"
said Miss Faye.

"I leap!"
said the swan.

And she felt like she was flying as the music played on.

After the performance, as the dancers all bowed,
Clapped the swan's beaming parents with the rest of the crowd.

"Bravo!" called the swans.

"Bravo!" called the crowd.

So they clapped and they cheered and they felt very proud.

Over in the meadow where the fireflies play
Sat the tired little swan with her teacher, Miss Faye.

"Done!"
said the swan.

"Well done!"
said Miss Faye.

"And I hope you'll audition for our big spring play!"